W9-BLW-426

What's a Pair?
What's a Dozen?

Stephen R. Swinburne

Boyds Mills Press

Foreword

From the moment you wake up until it's time to go to bed, your day is filled with numbers. Where's my pair of socks? How many waffles should I eat? Oh no! The school bus will arrive in a couple of minutes!

Numbers help us keep track of things. Although it's not always easy to find a matching pair of socks in your sock drawer. Can you imagine a world without numbers? How would you tell time? How would you count your toes? Numbers help us make sense of our world.

Knowing how to count up to ten is exciting. Learning number-related words such as single, pair, odd, even, and dozen can also be great fun. You may know some of the math words in this book; some you may not. Once you learn them, you can find numbers everywhere. Happy counting.

—Steve Swinburne

Everything starts with one.

A single ball is one ball.

If you are first in line, you are before all others.

The prefix uni- means one or single. A unicycle is a
bike with one wheel.

When you have two of something, you have a pair.

A couple also means two,
such as a couple of fire trucks.

Second and double are other words for two.
If you are second in line, you come after the first person.

The prefix bi- means two.
A bicycle is a bike with two wheels.

The prefix tri- means three. A triangle is a shape
with three sides and a tricycle is a bike with three wheels.

Triple and third are other words meaning three. This third grader is eating a triple-scoop ice cream cone.

If you have several hats,
you have more than two or three.

Some gardens have only a small number of flowers.
They have few flowers.

Some gardens have a large number of flowers.
They have many flowers.

Some games have an odd number of friends.

Some games have an even number of friends.

A half dozen is six. Half dozen is in between
or in the middle of a dozen or twelve.

A dozen is twelve.

A baker's dozen is thirteen.

Can you find the pair?

Which one is the unicycle?

Who's first in line?

Is this an odd or even number of friends?

Odd.

Is the juggler juggling a dozen
or half-dozen rings?

Half dozen.

One and one make two.
Sometimes that's just the right number.

To the dedicated and inspired teachers and assistants of Flood Brook Union School, Londonderry, Vermont, and West River Montessori School, South Londonderry, Vermont.

Acknowledgments:

Many thanks to all my patient models who stood by while the photographer fussed with lenses and film and waited for the right light: cover (from right to left): Hayley Swinburne, Colby Ameden, Mollie Wright, Caleb Ameden, Anna Wright, Darrien Clifton, Devon Swinburne, Riley Ameden, Jessica Brown, Taylor Brown, Robert Black and Alex Palmer; back jacket: Taylor Brown and Darrien Clifton; Gordon and Dylan McNair; West River Montessori School kids; kindergarten class at Brattleboro Central School; children from the Londonderry, Vermont, Farmer's Market; Aimee Bailey; Angel Fullard; Katie Streeter; Jocelin and Elisha Ruiz; and Russell Davis (juggler). Special thanks to Vermont farmer Jon Wright for cajoling a pair of cows for the jacket.

Published by Caroline House • Boyds Mills Press, Inc. • A Highlights Company
815 Church Street • Honesdale, Pennsylvania 18431
Printed in China

Publisher Cataloging-in-Publication Data
Swinburne, Stephen R.
What's a pair? what's a dozen? / by Stephen R. Swinburne. 1st.ed. • [32]p. : col. ill. ; cm.
Summary: An introduction to number-related words.
Hardcover ISBN 1-56397-827-X
Paperback ISBN 1-56397-871-7
1. Mathematics —Juvenile literature. 2. Number concept—Juvenile
literature. [1. Mathematics. 2. Number concept.] I. Title.
510 —dc21 2000 AC CIP
99-63097

First edition, 2000
Book designed by Randall Llewellyn • The text of this book is set in Garamond Light

10 9 8 7 6 5 4 3 2 1 hc
10 9 8 7 6 5 4 3 2 1 pbk